Erotic Stories for Women

Sex on Vacation

Hot Romance Novels

Vivienne Dupont

Table of contents

Adventure on the high seas

Oceania. Even the name of the huge cruise ship sounded like a vacation. Six thousand five hundred passengers, plus a crew of at least another two thousand members. A truly floating city, but a very exclusive one. And a very unfairly distributed one.

I had always wanted to ride on a ship like this at least once. It had taken thirty-two years. Of course, I didn't dream of it as a baby. Although... why not? Couldn't it be that one was born with a certain longing? How else could it be explained that I, growing up in the Ruhr area, which was basically one huge city, actually always dreamed of the sea? Even more: of traveling to it?

Ok. I did not dream of going to sea now. I didn't want to become a sailor or sign on with a container ship. No, I wanted to go on a cruise ship, a dream ship. And maybe experience such a beautiful love story as in all these stories.

My father seemed to have known about it, more than I had been aware of. Even as I had stood at his deathbed time and again, I had never articulated in detail my dreams of such a trip. I simply knew I could not afford it. But my father had listened, recognised the nuances between the lines, perhaps my look. And remembered that I had not formulated it only now, but always.

When my mother handed me the letter from my father after his death, the two tickets, I knew that he had listened to me all my life. However, he had probably assumed that I would go with Frank. He had been very fond of Frank and I had not had the heart to confess to my father that Frank had left me.

Yes, from a certain point in time I had always imagined myself and Frank to make such a trip - me and my dream prince on my dream ship. But that was it. A dream. Well, at least one part I would fulfill now.

"Thank you," my lips formed as I stood on the pier after all the checks and looked up at this massive ship. It was simply beautiful. 19 floors. On the top, three pools. Countless bars, sun decks, lounge chairs and restaurants. And all inclusive for me, as my father had booked me the truly premium option. There was more to it, but already this was more than I could ever dream of.

"This is so cool!", Nina shouted a little too loudly for my liking and pressed me against her, beaming with joy. She almost jumped up and down for sure, but I was just able to stop her.

"We'll sunbathe every day, sip cocktails, go out for super food, and then pick up guys. A different one every night. Or two. Not averse to it."

No, Nina was certainly not averse. Never been. And so she was of course not averse when I asked her if she would come along. Perhaps I should have sent her this offer in writing, since my ears were still ringing from her shrieking.

Nina was, unlike me, faster, more spontaneous and more intense. She did me good and was certainly in this situation exactly the right companion, even if I could not really imagine this at the moment, she drew far too much attention to herself and thus to us for my liking.

"Don't make such a face," she said, pulling me up the gangway. "This is going to be great."

I smiled, took a breath and nodded. My eyes sparkled and my smile would not fade as we walked through the ship. It was truly a dream, beautiful. And what also delighted me was all the people who looked similar to us, especially the children.

Since our luggage had already been taken to the room, we decided to explore the ship, deck by deck. At least the areas that were allowed for passengers, because there were of course also areas where this was not allowed.

Six restaurants. In addition, another eight, which were not inclusive, at least not for all, but in which you were also allowed to eat, but then you had to pay. Unless you had a father who had also booked these for you.

Even in the normal ones, the food looked delicious. How was I ever going to eat that much to justify my father's investment? Above all, was that what anyone wanted? What woman who wanted to lie down to sunbathe would fill her belly like that? That would make you feel bad every day, or eventually, screw it. Fortunately, there were also fitness rooms, where I guess you could work it off your conscience.

Nina took a pragmatic view. "We have to eat our way through all the restaurants once. Then we'll just screw the extra pounds back down. If you're not decadent here, where are you?"

Somehow she was right. While I admired the equipment around us, she already checked off the male passengers and the staff, whereby she certainly also caught the eye of one of the women.

Nina was not really to be overlooked either. Blessed with a physique that was socially considered extremely attractive, she was also not stingy with her charms. Light blond, short hair, which she had modelled on the satirist Lisa Eckart, an equally slender face of a classic beauty, which continued in her body. Large, round breasts, endlessly long, shapely legs and a truly enviable butt.

I was never envious of Nina, why should I be? I never sought her level of attention from others. While Nina couldn't attract enough attention, one was enough for me. Frank had given me that look and for a long time I had been able to hold that look. But then he had looked around and probably realised that other mothers also had very beautiful daughters who were not so prudish.

It was true, I could not deny myself a certain prudery. Why then had I chosen Nina, of all people, as my best friend, through whom my prudery became all the more apparent? Well, you can only really choose your friends yourself to a certain extent. In reality, life cobbles them together for you, and I couldn't have imagined a better one.

I wasn't really average either. I liked my face, which was not only roughly reminiscent of Molly Ringwald, but everything about me. And Molly Ringwald was the heartthrob of all those who had been teenagers in the eighties. Only the generation after that didn't really know who she was and what she had meant to the girls and boys. So when someone saw me, I probably didn't remind them of her, and so I wasn't as interesting as I would be if we were all living twenty years earlier.

Sometimes I liked my curly red hair and my rather pale, freckled skin, sometimes not. Since I did not get many looks anyway, I could not care.

But I felt that I was not as averse to Nina's uninhibited attitude to sex as usual. The sex between Frank and me had been good. But it lacked something special, which is why it was no wonder that he left me.

At some point in a relationship, people felt that sex should be something normal, something taken for granted. Sex just…happened. Not 24/7, because that would be sport, but there should be 24/7 opportunity. As a teenager, didn't you do everything you could to have sex? Didn't you take advantage of every opportunity? And then how great was that? That magic eventually gets lost if you're not careful. And that's exactly what happened with Frank and me. There was no longer any magic in our sex, it just happened without us knowing why.

As I stood at the railing looking out to the sea we would soon be launching into, I vowed to have a sensual adventure on this trip, if not several. I resolved to be more open. More erotic. More sensual. And not to always question everything. To make sure I enjoyed more.

10

I looked around. There were enough interesting men. And out of curiosity and fun I also looked at women, but did not really consider it. I had already done it once with a friend, or rather she with me. It had been long ago and of course beautiful, but also not what I wanted. I wanted a man.

When I looked around, Nina had no problems to choose someone, but here were some well-built gentlemen of creation present. I had to admit that these were nice to look at, but just did not arouse my interest. Yes, I wanted to engage in erotic adventures, but not at any price. Sex for the sake of sex, no. But I did not have to make my choice now.

Although...

As I let my eyes wander, a face already caught my eye. At first I thought Keanu Reeves was sitting at the bar in his role as *John Wick*, but on second glance it quickly became clear that it was neither. But there was a resemblance, especially the really nice smile he gave me...

Our cabin was a dream. We had not only a wonderful double bed, but also a space in between with something like a couch, which almost looked like a four-poster bed, and also a balcony. The bathroom was smaller, but perfectly adequate.

"I want to fuck at least once in this bed," Nina announced. "And on the four-poster bed. On the balcony, not so much. I'll leave that one to you."
I smiled. "How generous."

Immediately we unpacked our things, and I noticed that Nina seemed to own only clothes that came straight from the erotic catalogue. Everything was transparent, sinful red, lace, tight cut, generously cut to show a lot, low in fabric. The very next moment she undressed, stood briefly in the shower, and then put on a bikini that, if it had been a movie, would have been intended only for adults and even then would have been safely cut. Nina looked like the embodiment of sin itself in it and I thought it was wonderful. She also put on a colourful, quasi-transparent poncho and simple flip-flops. When she also smeared herself, which made any visible skin shine, it was clear to me that all attention would be on her.

Before we left the cabin, Nina paused once more and took a condom out of a package to put it in her bikini briefs.

"You should never be unprepared," she explained. "I always have one in my panties, too. Then when a guy takes it off me, he finds the right one to put on right away."

I finally decided to be brave and chose a bikini myself, which harmonised well with my red hair, but my body didn't look nearly as seductive in it as Nina's did. But I didn't care, because I could sunbathe in peace, while Nina was basically permanently flirting. I was amused with large, dark sunglasses camouflaged and with closed eyes, how Nina managed to make even harmless words sound like sinful utterances. So it was no wonder when she then took off with one and more or less headed straight for a locker room.

I smiled and continued to enjoy the sun. At the same time, I had the vague feeling of being watched. If one was normally not so often in the focus of attention, then this was ever more noticeable.

I didn't want to expose myself and look around, so I just lay motionless and hoped that I wasn't sending a signal to be approached. According to Nina, wearing a bikini was already the unmistakable signal to be addressed. However, she also emphasised that it was an even clearer signal if you wore nothing at all.

Nobody spoke to me and so the first day passed uneventfully. In the evening it was actually planned that the ship should leave, beautiful at sunset. Unfortunately, this had to be postponed, because some fliers and thus passengers had delayed.

I felt this was a great pity. Nina didn't care, she was already having a great time. This led to the fact that she said goodbye after the really successful welcome show, to walk away with a truly handsome southern-looking man smiling. Understandably so, because with the amounts of food she had squirrelled away, she was going to have to do quite a bit to work it off again. The man looked like he could help her do just that.

I did not feel like sitting alone among so many couples and went into the cabin. I looked up at the sky, where the moon and the stars showed themselves in incredible clarity. In addition, it was still, a beautiful mild summer night, which invited in every way to more. If Frank were here now, I would not have minded enjoying this night with him, united in breathless passion.

I had to smile. Yes, I really felt like having sex. But to have this now only with my hands, I found then but rather sad. Even my vibrator, which I had taken with me for God knows what reason, would not satisfy my actual longing. I wanted to be touched by hands and fingers that were not mine. And be kissed, caressed, massaged, wanted and taken. And not only in my imagination.

I put on my sinful red silk negligee, which was actually also too bad to wear for anyone, but it was so wonderfully cool on the skin. I also really liked how I looked in it and how I felt in it too. It went just barely over my butt, so of course I wore matching briefs with it, because otherwise the insights would have been too deep after all. In addition, it emphasised my legs and made them appear longer than they actually were. Or they were so long and I did not see it.

Thinking of Nina, I slipped a condom into the cuff of the panties. It might be crazy, but it felt good and made me smile.

Time passed and I heard the noise outside becoming quieter and quieter and finally falling completely silent. It seemed unbelievable, but this ship, which in the evening still resembled a big party, came to rest completely.

I enjoyed the sound of the waves and didn't realise how long I had been listening. Then, all at once, I noticed a change and realised that we were leaving.

It only took a moment for me to grab my bathrobe, along with the obligatory cabin card that not only opened it but was also used to pay for everything here, and sneak outside. No one was in the corridors, so I made my way to the deck, eventually going all the way to the front. There were still privacy screens here, so I felt safe.

It was a beautiful sight. The starry night. The lights of the city and the other ships. And ahead, the vastness of the sea that now awaited us with all its promise. I slipped off my bathrobe, just let it sink to the floor and closed my eyes, enjoying the sound of the waves.

"Excuse me," I suddenly heard a melodious voice. Startled, I turned and looked into the friendly smiling, full-bearded face of Keanu Reeves. Not the real one, but it was getting pretty close.

The man who owned it was lying on one of the numerous deck chairs and I had obviously overlooked him when I arrived.

"I didn't want to scare you, and now I have done just that," the man said. "But I didn't know how to draw attention to myself without startling you. However, when you began to undress, I thought it would be appropriate to call attention to my presence."

At first I was confused because I still had to process that he was sitting there. But then I smiled, too. "Very obliging. But just for the record: I wouldn't have taken my clothes off any further. I just wanted to enjoy the warm air."

He nodded and stood up to come to me. I swallowed involuntarily. Was he going to kiss me? No idea where the thought came from, but it was just there.

He looked deep into my eyes and smiled. "I'm Ben."

I caught myself again, but did not let his eyes leave mine. "Pleased to meet you. I'm Klara."

16

"Pleased to meet you Klara."

With that, he seemed to be eyeing me, but only my face. I had refrained from picking up my bathrobe and he refrained from looking lower than my chin. On the one hand I found this very impressive, but on the other hand it also irritated me. After all, here I was in a sinful negligee designed for a man to look closely at. And I knew he hadn't missed it. He didn't even ignore it, he just passed over it because he wanted to be friendly, a gentleman. Which, at the moment, I didn't want to have.

I know it sounds weird, but at that moment I didn't want a gentleman. Okay, yes. But a gentleman who wasn't one now. If that makes sense.

Maybe Ben would still do me the favour, but at the moment he was behaving far too exemplary.

"You remind me of someone," he said, continuing to look me in the eye.

I smiled. "I think I can guess. But I'm surprised you even know her. After all, like me, it was after your time."

"I'm a big movie fan. And her movies were on TV. I have the DVDs, too. She was my first, great love."

I laughed. "That's what it sounds like."

"After her, there was no one quite like her. Julia Roberts was once interpreted that way, but Molly Ringwald is as unique as Marilyn Monroe."

"Wow, those are big words. Marilyn is already a brand."

"So was Molly."

I nodded and then raised my right eyebrow mockingly upward. "You also know that you look like someone."

Ben laughed. "Yeah, I know. Not exactly the worst comparison. But I stress, I wore the full beard before."

I laughed. "Here we are, the two movie stars. And what are we going to do now with the night that has begun? The deck seems to be ours alone. So does the sea."

"Are you going to go all the way to the front and do the king-of-the-world act?"

My eyes became slits. "I hadn't thought of that"

He smiled. "I would have been surprised, too, with your getup. I rather assumed you were expecting someone."

I smiled. "I guess so."

18

"Then I guess I'd better recommend myself."

With that, he really bowed. I could not believe it.

"What if I waited for you?"

"In those clothes?"

I nodded.

He smiled a wonderful smile.

"And what were you going to do in it?"

Now I truly left behind my fear that always captivated me and decided to just jump.

"Let's find out."

With that I overcame the last bit between us and kissed him. Inwardly I just prayed *Please don't let him flinch*.

But he did not. Instead, he took my kiss and intensified it. Already he wrapped his arms around me and pressed my body against his.

If I hadn't been warm to the touch before, it would have been now at the latest. A shudder ran through my body and very briefly my knees felt like jello. How cliché, but yet so wonderful.

Something exploded inside me, as if all the chains that have always kept me at a distance were broken and I finally just broke free. My desire and passion, which had been restrained for so long, broke free and flooded everything.

Every fibre in me was screaming to finally unite with Ben. The later came later. And even though I couldn't believe what I had done then, now was now and all was well.

And Ben understood. His hands explored my body. First my back, then they moved forward. Oh, how good his hands felt on my breasts. They were still separated from his skin by the silky fabric, but it felt so good.

Between my legs I felt a pulling sensation that I hadn't felt with such intensity in a long time.

I pushed Ben back and smiled when he bumped his legs against the sun lounger. He sat down on it, but I continued to direct him so that he finally lay down and left everything else to me.

Directly I tugged at his belt and opened to free his member.

Smiling, I let my hand slide up and down his erect shaft. Where I suddenly possessed so much sexiness, I did not know. Maybe it was always there or I was simply schizophrenic and just left the field to my other personality.

Whatever it was, I didn't care. I enjoyed every moment. Enjoyed how Ben's member felt in my hand. Enjoyed the way he looked at me.

Finally, I reached into my panties and took out the condom. For a moment he seemed puzzled, but said nothing.

Like a pro, I opened the package and slipped it over him, then sat on him. I pushed aside the fabric of my noticeably wet panties and when I felt Ben's glans against my labia, it was like a lightning bolt that jolted through my body. I shuddered blissfully and finally settled down on him.

To feel him very deep inside me was just unbelievable. On the one hand warm and comforting, on the other, it seemed to me as if my desire was only now really ignited.

I lowered my pelvis very low, I truly wanted to take him completely into me. And then I moved. I let my pelvis circle, fast, violently. And it was good. So good.

Ben first held me by the hips, then let his hands wander to my breasts and knead them gently, then more eagerly, which only increased my lust.

I slipped my arms out of the straps, so that now my breasts were exposed and he could touch them directly. To feel his hands now without the barrier between them was even more delicious.

I moaned. Loudly. Audibly. And yet I was sure that only Ben would hear me, because the waves drowned out everything.

Oh, those waves. The sea with its incomparable sound was the perfect background to this moment. Never before had I dared to do something like this. Never let myself fall so easily. And now everything was perfect.

More and more I let my pelvis gyrate. Fed by an unknown force, I was completely my sexual self, which I always wanted to be. Not like Nina. She was her and all of herself. But I was me now finally as I had always dreamed. I was here and now the woman of my most erotic dreams. And Ben corresponded only too much to the dream man, whom I met there always connected in passion.

Faster and faster my pelvis circled, moving completely uncontrollably. I moaned and groaned. In my head, the sound of the waves became louder and louder, washing over my mind until suddenly a surge of emotion slammed against it and tore everything.

Loudly I moaned my orgasm into the so wonderful night, while my body trembled uncontrollably. Ben held me by the hips again, otherwise I might have just fallen off. It would have been a memorable exit.

Laughing, I looked down at him and he laughed as well.

"Interesting," he finally commented. "Is this how you usually first meet?"

I laughed. "I could tell you things."

"I'm sure and excited about that."

I nodded. "Molly never did anything like that in her movies."

He nodded as well. "Not in the ones in the eighties. In the later ones, something like this happened."

"Interesting. Then surely you couldn't have been that shocked at what I was doing here."

He smiled and stroked my still aroused nipples that it made me shiver again.

"Nothing you do can shock me. But I'm curious to see how the rest of the voyage goes. And whether you always do something like this when the ship leaves a port again."

I laughed, then looked at him. "Sounds like a good ritual, doesn't it? Repeat this every time we go out. And I'm sure we'll think of something for the time in between."

Ben smiled. And the way he looked at me, the trip promised to be an auspicious one. Thanks to Molly.

Fantasy Island

Eva went directly to the beach as soon as she had checked into the hotel. Already when she felt the sand under her feet, it was an incredibly wonderful feeling that moved through her legs to her head.

She was there. Really there.

The separation had been hell. It was clear that it had to happen when the wedding date was postponed yet another time. Yes, they both had to work and had their careers in jobs where something could always come up, but if you wanted to get married, you could. At least that's what she had believed.

Eva didn't know which of them it had bothered more to be engaged, her or Thomas. Maybe they would still be together if they had never decided to get married. Above all: decided. It had been more of a common sense decision, no different than the contracts they always negotiated in their respective professions. At the time, it had seemed truly reasonable to her. But now she knew that something crucial was missing.

The realisation had truly hit her like a hammer. The moment she properly realised the separation, everything, truly everything - her life, her attitudes, her views on the profession, everything - had collapsed like a house of cards. She had always thought this was an exaggerated notion, but now she knew what it meant.

At that moment, she knew only one thing: she had to get away. Not only away from Thomas, but also away from her life. She felt as if she had spent the last years of her now thirty-five-year-old life in a kind of bubble that had prevented her from ever waking up. As if she had been in a trance and had simply carried on without recognising the madness in it.

Everything that was important had been missing. She had not lived, she had existed. Everything had been deprived of meaning, of sensuality, so that she felt only a great emptiness when everything ended. Not because Thomas had filled her up so much, but because there was nothing, there was simply nothing.

Maybe others would have accepted it that way, but not Eva. As soon as she felt this emptiness, she booked a flight and packed her bags. Less than six hours later, she was on a plane that would take her to the Maldives. A few photos had been enough to make her realise that this island paradise was exactly what she needed to fill her emptiness.

The sun, the beautiful, soft sand, the water of the sea, everything was perfect. Eva simply walked into the water and when it touched her feet, it was like a baptism and a release of all the ballast that she had been carrying around for far too long.

For quite a while she just stood there, enjoying the feel of the water around her feet, the smell of the sea and the sand, and the warming sun on her skin. This was truly a paradise. But when she looked around, she saw other vacationers close by, some of whom eyed her suspiciously.

That wasn't quite what she wanted. But she also didn't expect to be alone.

Eva walked along the beach and noticed that she was still wearing her black skirt and white blouse that she had worn to work. Basically, she didn't care, but here she was already attracting attention and attracted even more glances. Not exactly what she wanted right now.

She looked around and her eyes found a small island that was a bit away from the beach, about a kilometre. There were palm trees and bushes and apparently a small beach.

"You can go there if you want," she heard a voice behind her. It belonged to an old man, a pensioner Eva guessed, sitting on a sun lounger and smiling kindly at her.

"Just go there?" Eva was confused.

The man nodded. "Yes. The water is shallow right now, just ankle deep. You can just hike over there."

Eva smiled. "Do I look like I need this?"

The old man took in the smile. "Who wouldn't need an island to themselves now and then?"

Eva nodded and started walking. At first she could not believe that this should be true, but the water was and remained really very shallow.

On the way, she pulled her blouse out of her skirt, unbuttoned it, and then tied it in front of her chest. Likewise, she gathered the skirt a little, because she still assumed that the water would be a little deeper, but it went to her at most well below the knees.

Walking a kilometre through water on sandy ground was no problem for Eva. She had always kept fit, not excessively, but enough. Even the long bike rides on the weekends had done their part to ensure that she still had well-proportioned legs. Her belly had only an imperceptible little bulge and her large, round breasts with their rather small atria continued to defy gravity. Her long blond hair was tied in a simple braid and she would have liked sunglasses for her dark blue eyes. In general, a bikini with a pareo would have been just the thing now.

When she reached the island, she felt like a conqueror and happy. And when she looked over the deserted beach and then looked back, she truly felt like she was in paradise. This was simply beautiful.

Eva let herself sink into the sand in thoughtfulness and simply listened to the sounds of the waves. As she spread out in the shade of several palm trees, she suddenly realised how tired she was and closed her eyes. The very next moment she was asleep.

When she opened her eyes again, she looked into the bright blue glowing eyes that were set in a tanned face framed with a full brown and grey beard.

Eva startled and looked at the man in disbelief. He looked like a castaway with his untrimmed, curly hair, his faded, unbuttoned Hawaiian shirt revealing a tanned belly, under which an old pair of short brown cargo pants could be seen.

"Well, look at that," the man said with a friendly smile. "Did you somehow take a wrong turn from a party?"

Eva looked at him in confusion. "Excuse me?"

The man pointed at Eva. "Well, your outfit. What are you? Lost tourist?"

Eva felt a little offended by this. "No. I went here to be alone for a bit."

"Ha," the man just said. "Yes, sometimes a few people come here. So the locals have also built a toilet house and a chest with the most important supplies. Always keep them in good repair, which I think is very nice. Because if you're stuck here, then you might need something."

Eva's confusion only increased. "Stuck? You can just go back over there, can't you?"

With that, she stood up and was about to leave when she noticed that something was wrong with the water. This included the fact that the island's beach had become much narrower.

"They could just walk over there a moment ago, it was still low tide," the man explained. "But now the water is back and it's evening. I wouldn't recommend you do that."

30

Eva turned around gruffly, "And why not? I'm a very good swimmer."

The man smiled. "I'll take your word for that, and I don't question it. But there's the matter of the sharks."

Eva was silent for a moment. "Sharks?"

The man nodded. "Yes. They're actually quite peaceful. But accidents do happen. They are just curious and when they go hunting in the evening sometimes a bit hot-headed. As I said, nothing major has happened so far. It's not like *Jaws* or anything. But someone did get a nasty wound."

Eva looked out at the water, which glistened magically in the evening sun, and could actually make out a couple of shark fins.

"Well fabulous. So you're telling me that I'm stuck here on the island."

"Adam," the man said.

"What?"

"My name is Adam."

Eva laughed. "Your name is really Adam?"

Adam looked confused. "Yes?"

Eva shook her head. "It's just because my name is Eva."

Now Adam had to laugh, too. "Adam and Eva are in paradise. Even if not completely voluntarily. I am. You probably rather less."

Eva took a breath and sat back down on the floor, then looked up at Adam. "Well, I'm just a naive tourist who just booted over here right after she arrived, but why are you here, Adam?"

Adam smiled and sat down next to Eva. "I'm here entirely by choice. If you ask the locals, they'd say I own the island. Which isn't true. I'm here to write. I'm a writer. Adam Landy. Maybe you've heard of me."

Eva nodded. "Indeed. My ex-fiancé always loved reading your adventure novels. He said you were particularly good at describing exotic places, so you felt like you were right there."

Adam smiled. "It helps that I travelled a lot in my youth. I was lucky enough to see these places before mass tourism really took off. I also discovered this island back then and wrote my first story here. Then one day when I came back because I had writer's block and thought I'd give it a try here, everything looked different too. Fortunately for me, the island had remained as it was. Except for the outhouse and the supply box, which I consider a plus. But over there, things aren't what they used to be."

Eva nodded. "That's too bad."

Adam shrugged his shoulders. "That's just the way of the times. But as long as the island still exists here, everything is fine with me. I haven't really left the place since I came back then. All those *Jack Napir* adventure novels your ex-fiancé holds in such high regard were written here."

Eva looked around, "How?"

Adam laughed. "By hand. Or even by typewriter. I have a laptop in my apartment over there where I type everything up again and then send it out. But the actual novels are still created here very old school."

He laughed and Eva did likewise, then glared at him. "No more desire to go out there and visit those exotic places you write about and once saw for yourself?"

Adam smiled and nodded. "Yes, I do, but somehow I feel the need to stop doing this alone." He paused for a moment before continuing. "And what about you? Is the reason you waded through the water so easily because your ex-partner is, well, just an ex-partner?"

Eva smiled sheepishly. "Yes. But only in part. When we parted, I looked at my life and realised there was nothing there. Quite the opposite of your life. Yours is so full that you've been able to draw on it for years and write novels that inspire people to go to those places."

Adam shrugged his shoulders. "Which, unfortunately, is how I contribute to these being overrun. Well, more frequented than normal. But there are a few places I still know that few have seen because they haven't come into such focus yet."

Eva smiled. "I'd like to see those sometime."

Adam nodded with a smile. Then he seemed a little embarrassed.

"Is something wrong?", Eva wanted to know with an irritated smile.

"Well, I'm thinking about how to tell you that you have to sleep with me."

Eva's eyes got big and she laughed. "Please? I've never heard a pickup line like that before. Does it really work? Ever?"

Adam smiled wryly. "I wasn't hitting on you."

Eva raised her right eyebrow mockingly. "So-so. Fascinating. Not hitting on me. Now I feel a little insulted."

"No. It's just that even if you had a cell phone, there's no reception here. That's why the locals built all this, so you can spend a night here without any problems. It's just that it gets pretty chilly here on the island at night, and there's only a couple sleeping bags."

Eve looked at Adam, then laughed. "If I didn't know reality and that it's my own fault that I'm in this situation now, I'd be willing to assume you planned all of this."

Adam laughed. "I can certainly think up the most absurd plots, but even I couldn't have planned this ahead. Picking a tourist, speculating that she'll come to this island, then putting her to sleep until it's too late. And before that, create this island first. And get all the sharks. That effort alone."

With that, he looked at Eva with a smile. "Are you worth it?"

Eva's expression did not change. Then she came very close to Adam's face. "I am *The Fuck of the Century*."

She laughed out loud. "I must have gotten sunstroke." She waved it off. "I'm not even *The Fuck of the Week* or *Day*. Especially not *of the century.* "

Adam smiled in amusement. "Well, I could think of someone less attractive who could have ended up here."

Eva nodded her thanks. "And you haven't even seen me in a bikini yet."

"Oh, I can imagine."

Eva raised her right eyebrow mockingly again. "You picture me in a bikini? So-so."

"I'm a writer. It's my job to imagine things. With or without things. Not only have the descriptions of nature always been praised in my books, but the sex scenes have also been described as very authentic. I even got an award for that once."

Eva nodded and looked at the water. "Do you draw on experience there, too."

Adam grinned. "I wish I was a stud like *Jack Napier.*" With that, he clapped his hands. "And I'll fix us something to eat for now. Don't expect much, it's truly emergency supplies only."

36

Adam lit a small fire and Eva marvelled at how quickly night fell. The stars twinkled in the sky and made the fruit, bread and dried meat taste better than it probably was. Even the simple outhouse proved surprisingly comfortable. The locals had truly put effort and love into it and were not stingy with wonderfully soft toilet paper. The wash water was only in a bucket, but even that had something.

As Adam had predicted, it had become noticeably cooler. While Eva watched Adam simply remove his shirt and pants so that he wore only brightly coloured shorts, she unbuttoned her skirt and bra. She buttoned up the blouse again, which left her with an improvised nightgown, albeit a very short one. The last thing she did was undo her braid, so that her hair fell half over her face and down her back.

Eva smiled when she saw that certain sparkle in Adam's eyes that every woman wanted to see when she appeared in such an outfit. When Adam looked at her closely and swallowed, she couldn't suppress a laugh.

Almost shyly, Adam opened the sleeping bag, went inside and held it open for Eva. Nodding her thanks, she climbed in, turned her back to him and pulled the zipper closed.

"I hope you're warm enough," Adam noted.

Eva grinned, but Adam couldn't see it because she was looking toward the fire. "As far as I know, you have to be very close together for optimum warmth."

Without waiting for Adam's answer, she moved very close to him, and it did not fail that their bodies touched again and again. Finally, Eva brought her pelvis to rest just in front of Adam's. However, apparently not far enough.

Again she grinned.

"Is that a bone or are you so happy to see me?"

Eva could literally see Adam swallow.

"Excuse me," he brought out a bit brittle. "It's been a while since such a beautiful woman right by me... And then the sight of you just now... Normally..."

Eva silenced Adam when she reached behind her with her right hand and stroked Adam's shorts, first gently, then more and more firmly massaging Adam's member through the fabric. At the same time, she couldn't get the grin off her face.

"Oh, boy," Adam snapped. "Eva, you're going to get me in a lot of trouble."

"That's my job as Eva," she replied. "I get Adam into trouble and fleshly sin."

With that, she took her hand away and pressed her butt against his member so that it was right between her butt cheeks and gyrated her pelvis.

Eva could literally feel Adam's arousal getting bigger and much harder.

Before Adam knew it, Eva was pulling off her panties and opening her blouse to throw them out of the sleeping bag as well. Then she turned around, smiled at Adam and lay on top of him, finally kissing him passionately.

At first Adam did not know what happened to him. But then he also gave himself into the kiss and embraced her with his arms.

Feeling his strong arms on her naked skin felt simply wonderful to Eva. Any thoughts that this was completely crazy dissolved into nothingness and were replaced by pure certainty. This was the most right thing she had done in a long time. And that included just driving off and flying away.

Eva lay on top of Adam with her legs spread and his bulging member pressed against her lap. She continued to gyrate her pelvis and a shudder ran through her body.

The desire to feel him inside her increased more and more and finally became unbearable.

Eva finally unzipped the sleeping bag a bit and made more room for herself. Now she managed to sit upright on Adam, still with her lap pressed on his. She moaned as she did so, because that alone was so arousing that she couldn't help it. When Adam put his hands on her breasts and kneaded them passionately, there was no stopping her.

In their relationship, it was basically always Thomas who took the initiative, from whom everything started.

But now everything started from Eva and she enjoyed it. This is how it should be. No limits. No questions. This is exactly what she wanted and there was nothing to it. Yes, she had known Adam for just a few hours, but that didn't matter. It was right. And that's why it felt so good.

Eva gave herself completely to the moment. She was on a beautiful paradise island having sex with a wonderful stranger under palm trees. Could there be anything more glorious?

More and more violently Eva's pelvis circled, which surprised even her. The impulses and eruptions of feelings that ran through her body were as intense as she had never experienced. Already she knew she wanted to experience this again. Again. Again. And again.

Eva moaned, letting it all out. Her fingers clawed into Adam's thick, already greyed chest hair. In response, Adam pressed his fingers harder into Eva's breasts, which made her laugh out loud, where a wave of orgasm immediately ran through her body and made it tremble.

In her subconscious, Eva heard the waves that were now crashing against the beach in unison with her movements. To feel Adam inside her, everywhere, here, on this paradise and her finally free, so free, was an inimitable feeling.

When she felt Adam's body tense up and he came inside her, it was the ultimate moment of happiness for Eva. Only now did she realise how sweaty her body was and how heavily she was breathing. She laughed and sank forward to first kiss Adam's head and then slowly roll to the side into his arms.

For a while they both just lay there and Eva listened to the sound of the waves. From the hotels she heard music, only softly, but she had to smile. It was truly a perfect moment.

"Don't all writers have a muse who provides a certain creative atmosphere and sleeps with them as often as possible to stimulate creativity?"

Adam smiled. "Yes. That's right. Never have though."

Eva nodded. "Yes, you always had that island. But you felt that maybe it wasn't working so well anymore. That you need to get out again and go to these places that are so wonderful. So how about I come with you? As your muse. Or rather as the one who reminds you of this island so you can write the books you want to write."

Adam stroked Eva's arm. "That sounds wonderful. But what about your work?"

Eva made a feigned serious thoughtful face. "Let me think about it. Continuing to work from dawn to dusk every day, only to find out again at some point that you have no idea who you are. Or to travel around the world with a great writer and even greater man, to see the most wonderful places, to drift in them with him at best, and thus help him to invent entertaining stories for people, which help the just-named people to forget a bit their everyday life. Hm, how am I supposed to decide?"

Adam laughed. "When you put it that way. But in your thinking, it doesn't matter that I'm rich, does it?"

Eva shrugged her shoulder. "A poor poet couldn't afford me as a muse at all. After all, I am *The Fuck of the Century*."

Both laughed and kissed each other. Then Eva smiled and looked at Adam.

"Or better yet, *the fuck of your life*."

Adam stroked her face and then looked around the island. "This is truly the island where fantasies come true."

Eva nodded. "I have another one. Let's make sure this one comes true, too."

With that, she lay down on Adam and kissed him passionately.

An old love on the Adriatic Sea

Kristi. I had least expected her. I had thought of her again and again. How could I not? But I no longer expected to ever see her again. And now she was standing in front of me, still with that dazzling smile. Oh, how I had missed that smile.

Kristi had always been there.

Until one day she wasn't.

You can't really remember your childhood days, but I remember the first time I saw her at the school enrollment party for 5th grade. This girl with this long, white-blond top hair and underneath it almost completely shaved off on the sides around her head. And these incredibly blue eyes.

The girl who offered me the seat next to her without hesitation as I stood a bit lost in class, not knowing anyone because we had just moved to the city for the summer.

The girl with whom I grew up from then on and only did not see every day when we were on vacation and during these days I always realised that I was missing something.

And that I missed even more when one day she was really gone. The day after our graduation ceremony, where it happened.

That was almost sixteen years ago now.

Sixteen years and a lifetime.

Training. Start of work. Marriage. Children. I had experienced all that without her, which I could never have imagined. And now she was standing in front of me.

When Greta suggested that we should all go to Italy together, my heart said yes directly, but my mind said no. It was always like that in the last few years. Maybe that was exactly the problem between me and Dirk. We did things only with reason, but no longer with our hearts. It was clear to both of us, even if we didn't really say it, that we were only together because of the children.

Italy seemed like a really good idea. A spontaneous ten days on the Adriatic Sea in the beautiful hotel "Grenavé". All double rooms, close to the beach, all inclusive. Greta had always had her connections and since she was thirty-five, she saw this as the ideal time to take a really nice girls' vacation.

"You do that," Dirk had said, smiling encouragingly. "I'm sure you could use it. And I'm sure my parents would be happy to just have the kids to themselves for a change."

That was true. For a long time, they had been planning to drive through France to Spain in a motor home with just their two grandchildren. And the children just loved the idea of being alone on the road with just grandma and grandpa, who spoiled them rotten. It really seemed ideal.

But wasn't that the beginning of the end?

Or was it the necessary break that everyone needed?

A breath to come up for air again so that one could continue?

Dirk took me in his arms and his smile was so wonderful. If he had told me like that that he was not having an affair with his colleague, I would have believed him. Alone, I knew better. I hadn't told him and I suspected that he didn't know that I knew either.

I could understand him. Such affairs happened when you no longer got the attention or inspiration you needed at home. Sex was not unimportant. Not only for the

46

satisfaction of basic needs, but also for the psyche and health. It was good and important for so many things. And we had simply lost ourselves in everyday life. Especially me.

As I stood on the beach in the glorious sunshine, surrounded by my friends whom I had known from school days, the worries at home seemed far away. They simply had no place here and that was wonderful.

Other worries came instead.

The beach was crowded with people in scanty clothing. Ultra-skimpy bikinis seemed to be especially trendy this year, truly worn not only by youth, but also by older people. It's strange when at thirty-five you could no longer count yourself as youth and felt old, even compared to other thirty-five year olds who were also here, showing off their tuned parts.

I had to admit that these overhauled bodies already looked good. And even though I knew that they only looked like this with the help of skilled surgeons, I was ashamed next to them. Yes, these bodies had been helped. But even if they hadn't, I'm sure they would still look great.

Yes, I had had two children. So what? I always found this excuse inappropriate. The children were not the only excuse for not exercising enough and eating too much of the wrong things. No, I could have done more. Dirk's affair also had two children, but she regularly pursued sports activities, was employed and took care of her children. And my husband, but that was another matter.

I was glad I had my pareo with me. It would cover most of my *problem areas*, the swimsuit the others.

What I liked about myself was my brown, long hair. It still shone like in my youth. Somehow I had paid more attention to it than to the rest of my body, for whatever reason. Maybe because I had always seen it as something special, while I saw the rest as rather very average.

Greta had said we had three double rooms, but there were five of us and I didn't have a roommate.

"Do I actually get a double room to myself?"

Greta smiled, though I didn't quite know if it was at me or at a group of men whose bodies all suggested that they had sworn off all sugar and fats.

"I have a surprise for you."

"Oh, come on. And which one?"

48

With that, her beam widened and she nodded to a vague point behind me. I turned around irritated and my heart stopped.

Kristi.

It hit me like a shock.

There Kristi came up to us. Older, but still with the same hairstyle, that smile and those green eyes.

Greta put her hands on my shoulders and was happy to be surprised, while Kristi came closer and finally stood in front of us.

"Hello," was all she said, which confused my mind even more than it already was.

"When I got the idea for the girls' vacation, I went looking for her," Greta explained. "And what can I say? I found her. And since I know you guys used to be really thick and probably have a lot to talk about, the last double room is for you."

I could only look at Kristi and didn't know what to say. She, on the other hand, just smiled. She probably saw my insecurity, but she wasn't laughing at me. Rather, she was apparently happy to see me, while I didn't know what I was feeling at all. I was just completely confused.

"I'll leave you to it then," Greta said. "After all, I heard your life story live, and Kristi told it to me when I found her again."

With that, Greta laughed, winked at us, and disappeared to join the others, who were chatting at the bar with some good-looking men.

There we were. Kristi and me. On a beautiful beach of the Italian Adriatic. All around us, people were enjoying life. Our girlfriends were flirting. Children were playing. The sand was glorious. The sun was shining, bathing everything in magical colours. It was beautiful and exactly how one could only imagine a vacation day to be.

I perceived all that.

But at the moment, all of this was completely unreal to me. As if I was just in one of those hyper-realistic virtual realities. And a little voice inside me said that it was so, because this could not be true, was too crazy.

How long we stood there in silence, I didn't know. All the time I looked into Kristi's eyes and she into mine.

"I don't think it's so good if we stand in the sun for so long," Kristi said, breaking the silence. "I'd love for you to join me for a cocktail."

At first I said nothing, then I smiled uncertainly and nodded.

As if in a trance, I followed her to the terrace of our hotel and sat down across from her in one of the two wicker chairs that were wonderfully shaded. Kristi ordered two Virgin Coladas and looked at me again while I looked at her. She was still as beautiful as she was when she was a high school graduate. Long, now very tan legs, a slim, athletic figure, long fingers, and still the face of Scarlett Johansson, but not quite her voice.

"A lot of time has passed," Kristi said with a smile.

I smiled wryly. "Do you mean because I look so old?"

Kristi rolled her eyes. "That's not exactly what I was going to say."

I smiled conciliatory. "You've become even more beautiful."

I knew Kristi hated compliments about her looks even then, but it was true. She had truly matured like a fine wine, a very fine wine. She was truly beautiful.

"Why didn't you ever get in touch?"

After years, I was finally able to ask the question that was burning under my nails.

Kristi smiled, but I saw the sadness in her eyes. "Out of fear."

I furrowed my brow. "Out of fear? What were you afraid of?"

Again her smile remained mirthless and it looked as if tears were forming in her eyes. "Of you rejecting me. That's why I left right then. I just had to get away."

I snorted. "For fifteen years. More, actually."

Kristi nodded, then shook her head. "I can't explain it, except that I was scared. I've never been so scared. I just had to get away. I couldn't have stood it if you..."

I leaned forward. "And what has changed now?"

"Nothing. Inside I feel like running away. But when Greta called and said you were coming... I don't know."

I smiled, but didn't really know what to make of it. "You were always the bravest person I knew. And then you're afraid of being rejected by me? Of what?"

52

Kristi smiled, then looked at the sea before looking at me again. "The initiative was mine at the time. And as much as I wanted it, I realised later that I probably just blindsided you. You were my best friend, always had understanding for me. Jesus, I never would have made it through high school without you, and we both know it. I thought I was just taking advantage of your good nature. I felt terrible. But I didn't want to hear that you didn't feel the way I did. I couldn't have stood that."

I snorted and now also smiled mirthlessly. "Anything to say, I never had the chance. When I woke up, you were gone. And then I had to find out that you were really gone. I was still hoping that you would come back someday. But you didn't. No message. No letter. No information. Just gone."

Kristi looked down and nodded. Then she looked at me again, shaking her head. "I really didn't want to lose you. I was really trying to get this homosexuality fucked out of me. I thought if I just did it with enough guys, it would go away: exorcist-like. That I was just confused. But I wasn't. I've always been a lesbian. And my feelings for you didn't change either. And, I don't know, the night of our graduation party, everything was so perfect. The two of us sort of there as a couple because we didn't have a date, so we went together. The whole vibe. You in that dress. I was suddenly full of hope and believed I could cross the line I had set for myself. But when that happened, you were asleep and I was in the bathroom, I saw my reflection and it disgusted me. I couldn't bear what I had done to you, but even less could I bear your rejection. Therefore, I packed my things and disappeared."

I nodded. "And over fifteen years later, here you are."

She nodded as well. "Yes."

"And what did you expect me to do?"

Kristi smiled, but again the smile did not reach her eyes. "I didn't expect anything. I just wanted to apologise, even though I know there's no excuse. And no explanation either. I was just scared."

"For fifteen years?"

She laughed, then nodded. "Yes. You could put it that way."

"Did you have relationships during that time?"

"Yes. Some. But none have lasted."

I smiled wryly. "Did you always run away when things got serious?"

Kristi laughed. "Ouch. No, at some point I always noticed something was missing."

"And what was that?"

Kristi's smile softened. "You."

I took a breath and then looked out to the ocean. Then I looked at Kristi, who was once my best friend. With whom I had shared more than with anyone else, if not everything. Kristi, who I had thought was the bravest person ever. And the most beautiful. That the boys chased after her by the dozen, I could understand all too well. Even if she had never tried, she had always been beautiful. And now she was even more beautiful.

But I also saw her agony. I could see all too clearly that her inner doubt had not left her alone for fifteen years. I felt so sorry for her. And this feeling outstripped everything: pity. And from this was fed the feeling that had never disappeared in all those years and which was the reason why I thought of her again and again.

And this feeling also made me make my decision.

I had not been brave for so long. Had not relied on my gut feeling for ages, let alone my feeling itself. Everything was always only rational and concerned about security. But life was not safe. And didn't the best things happen out of rationally considered irrationality?

I've always liked the saying, "The heart has reason where reason knows nothing." When was this more true than now?

Suddenly everything was so clear and so easy.

I looked at Kristi, smiled, and finished my cocktail. Although it didn't contain any alcohol, it made me feel so exhilarated that I stood up and held out my hand to Kristi.

Kristi looked at me in confusion. "What are you going to do?"

"An experiment. Whether you can make up for fifteen years in ten days."

Kristi looked at me for a long moment. "Are you sure?"

I shrugged my shoulders. "What's for sure? All I know is that you shouldn't have gone. That was a mistake. But I certainly won't let you go again."

Kristi slowly stood up and finally took my hand. "You really are braver than me."

I smiled. "Actually, no. But for some, it pays to be brave."

Kristi nodded. "I'm so sorry about everything."

"And I'm sorry I didn't make you feel more like I would never let you fall."

With that, we went to the front desk and had them give us our room keys.

How it sounded: our room key. There was something crazy about it.

I felt Kristi's hand shaking and I had to smile. She had always been the strong one. I'd noticed over the years people around me were always so confident, even when everything indicated that they actually had doubts. But today it was me who had the initiative. Who was completely self-confident. Maybe later I would wake up from this bubble of courage and scream at the top of my lungs about what I had done without thinking much.

Our room was on one of the top floors. Actually, I did not like these tourist buildings. These bed castles in cities that had been artificially built solely because of tourism and had not grown naturally.

When we entered the elevator, two people got on and then got off on the second floor. As soon as the doors closed, I turned to Kristi and kissed her. At first she was surprised, then she kissed me back. Shortly before we reached our floor, I let go of her again.

"You're crazy," Kristi agreed.

I nodded and took a breath. "Yeah, for now it does seem that way. And I hope this craziness lasts for the next ten days, because that's what I want."

With almost trembling fingers, I unlocked the door to our room and we entered. As soon as we were inside, I locked the door and only then looked around. We had gone directly to the terrace and the beach when we started and hadn't even gone to our rooms yet. Now I had to realise that Greta had truly not let herself be lumpen.

The room was large, so we certainly didn't have to feel like we were constantly on our feet. Everything appeared new or truly just very thoroughly cleaned. The style was old-fashioned, with red walls and gold trim. The almost huge double bed was a real dream. The bathroom, on the other hand, was small, enough for one, but would certainly be a bit cramped with two. The shower in it offered only one really with enough space. Two, however, had to stand really close to each other.

Smiling joyfully, I turned around.

"Can you stand it here with me?"

Kristi looked like she was still waiting for everything around her to burst like a soap bubble right then and there.

"With you, I'd stand anywhere."

I raised my right eyebrow. "I'm sure there are worse places to put up with me than a four stone hotel all inclusive and right on the ocean."

Kristi laughed and then stepped very close to me. As she looked into my eyes, everything in me suddenly became totally soft and my brain seemed to want to lie down on absorbent cotton.

Before I knew it, our mouths met. Then there was Kristi's gentle tongue slowly pushing against mine. Slowly, but steadily, our kisses became more passionate. How Kristi pressed me against her body, it was an incredible feeling. Clearly I could feel her nipples, which apparently tried to pierce the fabric of her bikini.

My hands wandered to her pareo, pulled it over her head, to then also release her bikini top almost gruffly from her body.

When I looked at her breasts, I felt hot and cold. More than fifteen years ago I had seen them this way for the first time and now again. I put my hand on them and a shiver went not only through my body.

This was apparently the last signal Kristi needed, because now she took the initiative and took off my shirt and sports bra, which I had already sweated through completely during the trip.

In view of Kristi's so flawless body, I felt a little embarrassed. But when Kristi put her hands on my breasts and started to knead them, this thought disappeared forever.

With this, my last inhibitions, which I might still have had somewhere, also fell. My so long closed desire broke through and I kissed Kristi passionately.

Kristi's hands were everywhere. It was clear that she had much more experience touching a woman than I did. I let myself go with the flow and enjoyed the energy that was so unleashed.

Kristi took off my skirt and also had the grace to pull my panties right down with it, saving me the embarrassment of her seeing them. Nothing about them were sexy, as I hadn't expected to impress anyone either. My underlying shame, however, luckily I had completely shaved, as I always did when I went to the sea and wore bathing suits.

60

Kristi's head was now directly level with my so aroused womb and I was breathing heavily. Kristi looked at me, smiled and finally closed her eyes as she put my left leg on her shoulder and pressed her mouth on my labia.

Explosion.

That was it.

A single, magnificent explosion.

I could have cried, it felt so wonderful. But then Kristi ran the tip of her tongue over my clit and I moaned. An enormous shudder seized my body and I trembled as if I had been given electric shocks.

Involuntarily I reached into Kristi's hair and could just restrain myself from tearing at it. Kristi, however, seemed to be completely insensitive to pain, because she only pressed her mouth even harder on my pubic bone and sucked, sucked, licked it with pleasure.

My knees were on the verge of simply sagging away. But I didn't care. I was in heaven. Everything was good. Perfect.

Kristi, however, directed me around and let me sink down onto the bed. While my upper body was now up to my pelvis on the bed, my legs were still outside. Kristi immediately lowered her head again and gave herself completely to her passion and desires between my legs.

I did not know what happened to me. I moaned, sighed, wailed. Wanted it to never end.

The feelings, which incessantly ran uncontrollably through my body, were actually unbearable. I felt as if I could no longer stand it all. It was just too much. Much too much. But I could not let go of it, wanted to feel everything, more and more and more.

Then there were Kristi's fingers. Her long, so supple fingers.

I still remembered well the first time they penetrated me. Explored my innermost being. Everything. Now nuance. And touching points that made me think Kristi could play on my arousals like a piano. I was completely at her mercy and my brain was no longer capable of any normal thought.

That's exactly how it was now.

As Kristi pushed her fingers inside me, slowly, inexorably, deeper and deeper, twisting, I couldn't breathe. I just forgot about it. It didn't matter anymore. All that mattered was that Kristi's fingers were inside me. And what she was doing with them inside me. What she was making me feel.

Like a drowning man, I finally caught my breath again and then moaned all the louder. My fingers clawed at the bed sheet and I wouldn't have been surprised if I had just torn it. I even wished I had, because I wanted to show Kristi how good what she was doing to me was.

This was torture. It couldn't be anything else, because how could I ever live again without all that. It wasn't about sex per se. It was about experiencing this with her.

Kristi directed me higher into the bed and I followed. She had her left hand between my legs incessantly, penetrating me again and again with her fingers to massage my clit with her thumbs.

As she lay there beside me, a tear ran down my face. Kristi bent down and picked it up with the tip of her tongue, smiling. Then her lips laid on mine and we kissed passionately again, while Kristi's right hand now massaged my breasts as well. Finally Kristi leaned down and sucked on the other breast.

Everything passed me by. The rush of emotions was simply too great. And then everything exploded inside me. Again. And again and again. At the same time, it felt like huge waves, packed with the most incredible, wonderful, yet not really bearable feelings.

My body trembled incessantly and I was firmly convinced that I would have to die, since no human being could survive such emotions, no matter how good they might be. Fifteen years of pent-up emotions discharged all at once and simply washed my mind away, while I felt happier than ever.

"Wow," was all Kristi said when I was in her arms later. "That was intense. I can honestly say I've never experienced anything like it."

I smiled wryly. "It's not like you've ever let anyone die of thirst for fifteen years."

She smiled and stroked me through my sweaty hair.

"And what happens now?" she wanted to know. It sounded like a simple question, but I could hear her heart pounding. A lot depended on my answer for her.

I shrugged my shoulders. "For the next few days, you're going to give me everything you've been holding out on me. So we fuck like rabbits, so that I can no longer run."

She laughed. "Oh, I wouldn't mind if you did that to me, too."

"Later. Because there, too, fifteen years of fantasies have piled up that I'm only too happy to vent on you."

"Sounds tempting." She lowered her head and I lifted mine to hers. The kiss was long and loving.

"And then where do we go from there?"

Again her heart was hammering.

I smiled. "I guess I'm due for a talk with Dirk. I'm sure it won't be pretty. But basically, we both know our marriage is over. Now all we can do is make sure we're at least good parents."

Kristi was silent for a moment.

"Would you break up with him even if you hadn't met me again?"

I nodded my head. "Yes. It would have happened even without you. You're just giving me another reason. Dirk's not a bad guy. We were friends first, before we got together. Maybe that was the problem. Because I miss him as a friend. Does that make sense?"

Kristi nodded. I looked at her again, looked at her and stroked the index finger of my left hand over her face.

"Did you find a wrinkle?" she asked, smiling so wonderfully.

I nodded. "I would have liked to have witnessed you getting it."

Kristi's smile widened. "You'll see all my wrinkles yet to come."

"Promise?"

"I promise."

And with that, we kissed again. Long. Passionately. And then I showed Kristi one of my long-cherished fantasies with her.

Adventure in Australia

When you imagined the dimensions, it was just mind-boggling. Thousands of kilometres across Australia from the West Coast to the East Coast. Even with a plane, it would have taken a few hours, but with the train it took days.

For Tina, this was the fulfilment of a childhood dream. Which is why she introduced herself everywhere not as Christina, which was more fitting for a woman of thirty-eight, but as Tina, who still came from her childhood and youth. That simply fitted better. At home in everyday life, she was a businesswoman who earned her money in a medium-sized company. Christina Ewers. That belonged there, since a certain appearance counted and a Tina was more likely to fetch the coffee in these circles.

Tina was long past the point of fetching coffee. Not beyond the dreams she'd had as a teenager. Travelling the world had always been her greatest wish. To be able to make a living from it was an even greater one.

Unfortunately, she was born a little too late for that, at least that was her impression. Because nowadays, thanks to YouTube and all the other social media, such a thing was quite possible. How often had she spent her breaks watching videos on the various channels of people who were doing just that? Living Tina's dream life.

Perhaps she was also born too late. Her love of travel came up through the stories of her parents' friends. They had actually travelled through Southeast Asia in the sixties and had brought back photos and stories from there that were no longer possible today, when commercial tourism had changed everything.

So Tina has had the feeling more than once that she was born at exactly the wrong time. But the longing never died. And to satisfy it, she knew, she needed money. So what could be more obvious than to look for a well-paid job? She had also tried it once as a travel agent, thinking that she would get closer to her goal. Unfortunately, that was a bust, because the constant package tours she sold people had little to do with what she wanted.

And so she spent many years going to work in the morning, watching or reading just about every travelogue in her free time, dreaming, saving, and travelling to her places of longing on her vacations. But again and again she had the impression that it was too little.

Well, and then there had been her niece Sandra, who one day gave her a small digital video camera, plus a camera that could be attached to her head, and revealed that she had set up a YouTube and Instagram account for her.

"You just talk all the time anyway about all the places you should travel to and want to report on. Then do that too. Even people as old as you want to travel and perhaps not always be looked at by young, dynamic people who know how to present everything hip, but lack depth, maturity and experience. And probably also real longing. Maybe it's your reports that people have been waiting for."

And so, as an operator, Sandra sent her Aunt Tina out to finally live her dream at thirty-eight.

Tina had never felt as happy as she had in the last few weeks. She had been to India and had dared to do things she had only dreamed of. And the camera had always been there, along with a small laptop. She had also taken an old notebook with her, in which she was still writing, because of course she had a book in mind that she wanted to write.

At home, Sandra took care of Tina's site so that everything was in line with viewing habits but without hip bells and whistles. When Sandra told Tina that she had even arranged advertising deals, she couldn't believe it. But there were truly quite a few people who looked at the things Tina recorded and commented on, and commented on them again. Tina wasn't quite ready to admit to herself that the dream of making a living from travelling and reporting could come true. But it really looked that way, and more and more every day.

When Tina entered her own sleeping compartment, she had to smile. She would share this small room with someone else and sleep in something like a loft bed again after a long time. The bathroom was tiny and just big enough to turn around in. There were certainly more luxurious options, but this one was perfectly adequate.

What pleased Tina very much was that there was a large window where she could see the landscapes passing by. Landscapes that truly looked like they were from another planet and were simply impressive.

Tina put her large travel backpack in a corner and took off her thick tracking boots. As good as these were for all her undertakings, she was also glad to get rid of them every time.

The two beds were attached to the wall at the moment. They could be folded down and Tina wondered once again how they could stand it when you lay on them.

Finally, she got up, took a ready towel and the small shower gel bottle and went to the bathroom. Undressing was not so easy here, but somehow it worked, which she found quite funny. Just as she was taking off her sports bra, which she still didn't know whether it looked sexy or completely unsexy, she heard someone enter the compartment. This had to be her fellow passenger, with whom she would share the compartment for the ride.

"Hi, I'm Tina," she said through the door that was open a crack. "I'm taking a shower right now."

With that she threw out her shorts, shirt, panties and bra. "Sorry. It's a little tight in here and I don't want things to get wet. Otherwise, though, I'm actually pretty neat."

With that, she closed the door again and stood under the shower. The warm water was wonderful and she felt her entire body relax. This is exactly how it should be. She was also glad that she had decided to get herself some disposable razors at the hostel so that she could depilate herself in the crucial places, because she liked the way her skin felt now.

"You have to offer people something visual," she had admonished Sandra. "People would rather watch a beautiful, revealing woman doing what she does than one who is much too covered up. That creates distance. And travel and adventure also have something to do with permissiveness and eroticism. You don't have to walk through the jungle in a thong, even though I would love to see that. And so would the viewers. With your butt, you could easily wear that."

Tina had never been a prude. But she certainly wasn't the one who was all about permissiveness either. She didn't really think about it. In her job, which she hoped would soon be a thing of the past, there was a certain clothing etiquette that she also complied with. In her free time, however, she didn't want to think about it, even if something would be sexy, erotic or similar now. She wore short shorts and tight tank tops normally, because she felt comfortable in them. And when it got really hot, also her colourful bikini. Fortunately, this was exactly what Sandra imagined.

Tina smiled and looked at herself in the small mirror, which she wiped clean. She had become browner again and her hair even lighter. Also her green eyes sparkled more and in general everything about her was also tighter and more athletic.

She had always enjoyed sports, but not excessively. She just knew that if you wanted to climb a mountain off the beaten path, you needed a certain level of fitness. Thus, training was a means to an end. On her journey, however, her body was stressed all by itself and thus also shaped to the needs.

Her legs were much more well-proportioned, her buttocks firmer, as were her breasts, which were already one of the selling points for her niece anyway. Big enough that a male hand had good room on them and something to grab. Her smile also seemed more cheerful and open.

Tina wrapped the towel around herself, which was just enough to sparsely cover her upper body and pubic area, and entered the compartment with a smile.

And was irritated.

The young man standing in front of her was not a woman. She almost voiced this thought, but instead she just stood there.

"Hello, I'm Sydney," the young man, who couldn't have been more than twenty-five, said, raising his hand. "I think we'll share the compartment."

Tina was confused. "Are these unisex compartments now?"

Sydney smiled crookedly, and Tina had to admit that it was a nice smile. In general, Sydney was very handsome, as his clothes already suggested that he was also exploring the country. His hair was short, actually dark, but was light at the tips. He did not appear overly athletic, but fit. His skin was tanned, but not as much as Tina's, and his brown eyes radiated something trusting.

"I think there was some confusion at the time of booking because of my name," Sydney said. "I think they assumed I was a woman."

"But you're not?", Tina wanted to make sure.

Sydney laughed. "No."

"And you don't want to be one either? You're not transgender or something?"

Again Sydney laughed. "No, not that either. Just a guy whose parents thought it was unique to name their kid after their favourite city. And didn't consider possible problems. Doesn't happen to be for the first time that I'm mistaken for a woman because of my name. Unfortunately, I didn't consider that when I booked."

Tina nodded. "And the train is fully booked, that much I know."

"Looks like it."

Tina nodded again. "Well then, I guess we'll spend the trip together."

Sydney seemed surprised. "Doesn't that bother you?"

Tina opened her eyes. "Okay, wow. You're totally old enough. I'm older than you, yes, but hopefully not as old as your Mom."

Sydney smiled a smile that would have surely caused trouble for many a young lady. "Sorry. I was just being polite."

Tina smiled and shook her head. "And I'll throw my underwear at you first. Well, fabulous. Sandra will love that story."

"Who is Sandra? Your partner?"

Tina put a hand on her hip. "Ok, apparently we've both gotten past a certain point of inhibition. No, Sandra is my niece who sends me around the world to get stories for my blog or whatever you want to call it. And she would really like this one."

Tina raised her hand. "But now I have to find something to wear first. I wasn't prepared for a gentleman caller."

"And I don't mind, sharing the compartment with such a beautiful woman."

"Ah, a charmer."

"I could go outside for a minute," Sydney suggested.

Tina waved it off. "No, it's fine. We'll just unfold the beds and I'll lie down up there. That's what I was planning to do anyway. My feet could use some relaxation."

Sydney nodded and set about folding down both beds. Apparently, he knew his way around.

"Thank you," was all Tina said and slipped into bed upstairs, where she made a sound of comfort.

"You wouldn't believe how good that feels," she finally said. "The bed in the hostel wasn't quite as comfortable. This one, on the other hand, is fantastic."

Sydney smiled and then went to work on his backpack as well. "I'm going to go to the bathroom, too, then."

Tina just smiled and then looked after him. When she noticed how much she was looking at him, she rolled her eyes. Jeez, he was a real boy punt against her. A good-looking one, though. And how long had it been since she... A while. Which wasn't really a problem, since she had a satisfying selection of vibrators available at home. But travelling mostly off the beaten path? There was no place for such a thing. And what did she have her hands for, including her supple, flexible fingers?

76

Ok, she had really used them the last time in her youth, until she had spent her first really earned money in the sex store for a clitoral vibrator and a dildo. She could still remember what the first night with the two things was like. When it was over, everything felt sore as she had truly done it over and over again. She already thought she was a sex addict. Since then she had done it often and gladly with these and further added devices, so that her hand was not really used anymore.

She wondered whether she could still do it?

Sydney was really handsome. And for some reason, Tina's libido was going crazy. That's what happens when you're used to regular masturbation to relieve the pressure that builds up. No one had ever talked about this in the travelogues before. But there it was also mostly couples who then certainly drove it in the most exotic places, but of course did not report it. But she was alone.

How was she supposed to be in a room with Sydney all the time and not even really, well, release pressure? Did she have to do it in the shower?

Besides, she felt it now. What was she going to do?

Tina took a breath and rolled her eyes. Should she tell Sandra about this? Basically, such a thing was possible.

They had often talked about men and related topics. And this was really too amusing not to tell her, her niece had earned that.

Whether she reported about it in her blog, however, that was something else. Whereby a blog with the title "The most exotic places where you should fuck" would certainly be well visited. For singles travellers the alternative title "The most exotic places where you should masturbate". Maybe that was something under a pseudonym. And it was certainly fun.

When Tina heard the shower, she slid her right hand between her legs. The other she let slide to her breasts, pushing down the towel with it.

Even as her fingers spread her labia apart, it hit her like a bolt of lightning. And when Tina touched her clit, she had the feeling of sinking fully into the mattress. The feeling was so good and it felt to Tina as if a dam had broken. The excitement really flooded her and she moaned loudly.

Her fingers may not have been used for a long time, but they seemed to remember exactly everything. While her left hand kept kneading her breasts, wildly and tumultuously, her right hand massaged her most sensitive spot in a way that sent wave after wave through her body.

Tina didn't know where to put her legs, which were constantly moving. She arched her back, it felt so good, as she fantasised about Sydney taking her. Hard. Passionately.

Tina bit her lips, otherwise even the shower would not have drowned out her sounds of pleasure.

The shower.

Which no longer ran.

How long has it not run?

Tina opened her eyes and saw Sydney standing in the doorway to the bathroom. He looked at her, but Tina couldn't quite interpret his gaze.

"How long have you been standing there?" Tina wanted to know.

"How long have you been doing that there?" retorted Sydney.

"Well..." Tina didn't really know how to answer that.

"Let's get this straight: I'm taking a shower and you're masturbating?"

"Uh... yeah?"

"And at that, you made me..."

Tina was trying to get something out. She was always pretty good in meetings when someone tried to back her into a corner. Here, however, she couldn't think of anything. But attacking forward was probably the best defence here, too.

"So why didn't you make your presence known? Did you get off on it?"

Sydney appeared surprised. "If you want to put it that way, yes. I found it very arousing. I've never heard a woman moan like that before. Especially not over me."

Now Tina was perplexed. A thought formed in her head. A strange thought at first, outlandish. But the more she got involved with it, the more it seemed to make sense to her.

Carefully she got out of her bed. As she did so, she made sure to cover herself with the towel again as much as she could. Standing on the floor, she looked at Sydney for a long time, then turned around and folded her bed up so that only Sydney's remained.

Again she turned to Sydney and finally dropped the towel, so that she now stood completely naked in front of him.

Sydney looked at her. There was no lust or anything in his eyes, but true interest. As if he were looking at something beautiful. Tina knew this look, she had seen it on so many tourists looking at a natural or man-made wonder. But until now, no one had ever looked at her as if she, too, belonged to these wonders of nature.

"Are you sure?", Sydney wanted to know. Tina laughed, because isn't that the kind of question you ask when you're in bed with a virgin? Well, her sex life wasn't outstanding now, but she wasn't a virgin either.

Tina put her hands on her hips. "Actually, I would have every reason to be offended right now that you didn't pounce on me directly. But apparently you're still old school and a gentleman. That's kind of nice, but also weird. But if a woman undresses in front of you, then, my young one, that is exactly the statement that she is sure. And your job is then only to take her so violently that she loses her hearing and sight with pleasure."

Sydney smiled. "Understood, ma'am."

Tina nodded. "I hope you have condoms. It's a long drive and we're going to need a lot of condoms."

Sydney nodded, then looked thoughtful. "If need be, we could still pass the time with a quartet of diggers."

Tina raised her finger. "Don't push it, young one."

With that, she lay down in bed.

"Now get to it before I realise I must be completely out of my mind."

Sydney laughed and took off his shirt, revealing an official six-pack underneath.

Tina nodded appreciatively. "Okay, maybe the whole idea isn't so hare-brained after all."

Again Sydney laughed and now took off his pants.

"Weren't you going to take a shower?" asked Tina in light of the fact that Sydney was still wearing all of his clothes.

"Yep. But I always like to run water in front. And in the process, I realised I had forgotten the towel."

Tina nodded. "And when you came into the compartment..."

Sydney nodded. "Did I see something else coming."

Tina's face remained serious. "Understandable. Then don't let me stop you from undressing now."

Sydney laughed and then went to his backpack. As with everyone, he pulled out an incredible amount of stuff that once again made it seem like backpacks were bigger on the inside than the outside. Finally, he pulled out a pack of condoms. Not opened, as Tina noticed.

"How many are in there?" she wanted to know.

"Fifteen."

Tina made a dismissive face. "Well, let's see how far we can get with this."

Sydney laughed out loud and then came over to her. Tina would have expected a youngster like him to be nervous when he was about to have sex with a significantly older woman. But Sydney showed no signs. She was impressed by that. He, too, was apparently older on the inside than his appearance revealed.

Sydney smiled and leaned down to kiss Tina. A good start. As she did so, she felt him put his hand on her thigh and caress it there.

"Just so we're clear," she interrupted him. "I want to fuck you. I'm not a girl you have to coax first because she doesn't really know what she wants. I know exactly that. I'm very aroused and I want it. Now."

"Roger that, ma'am."

With that, his kiss became more passionate and his grip on her thigh tightened. His hand also immediately moved to the inside of her thigh. Much better already.

Now Sydney began kissing her neck and quickly working his way to her breasts. As he circled his tongue on her nipple, Tina moaned in pleasure. Then there was his hand and he kneaded it, sending a cascade of colourful flashes to her head. At the same time he put his other hand between her legs and his fingers parted her labia. Now he really went into full swing.

When he penetrated her with his fingers, Tina moaned loudly. She didn't even know how she had missed strange fingers inside her until she felt it now. It was just fabulous.

Sydney may still be young, but he truly knew what he was doing. Either he was a natural or well trained. Or Tina just too horny that she now reacted to everything violently.

Then suddenly Sydney's head was between her legs and his mouth was sucking her labia, her clit. Well, Holla the Forest Fairy.

Tina braced herself against the wall above her head with her right hand, held her breath, and then groaned all the harder. If she told Sandra about it, she would cut some parts.

Sydney seemed to be everywhere now. Tina's entire body was on fire and she felt like screaming. Was he really that good? Or did Tina just totally need it? She didn't care, but by now she couldn't wait for him to take her properly. To feel his fingers inside her was all well and good, but her sense, her body was calling for much more.

When Sydney stood up, she felt this as a huge loss. But when he took off his clearly baggy shorts and thus presented her his fully erect member, her anticipation increased immeasurably.

Smiling, he opened the condom packet and pulled it over himself. Then he lay down on top of her and Tina awaited him with her legs spread wide.

Finally he penetrated her. No games. Just one thrust and immediately more.

Tina moaned and groaned. After only a few thrusts she had her first orgasm and already another one was building up.

The force of his thrusts was incredible. They went through and through Tina. While she peripherally heard the rattle of the train, his pelvis slapped ceaselessly against her lap, the sounds of pleasure.

For Tina, it felt like he was not only fucking her body, but also her mind. She hadn't felt this good and this aroused in a long time.

Suddenly he slid out of her and turned her around. This was a bit awkward due to the lack of space, but also fun. And all the more exciting when he lifted her buttocks to now take her from behind with hard thrusts, reaching for her breasts and kneading them eagerly.

Tina moaned and groaned. Let it all out. Surrendered completely. Sydney didn't need instructions on how he could do it better. What he was doing, Tina was doing, and was exactly what she could only hope for. And with each thrust, it felt to her like he was hitting a new spot, as the pulses were just insane.

Again an orgasm made Tina's body tremble while Sydney didn't stop pumping into her.

How Tina would have liked to feel him coming inside her. But safety came first. But the desire for it was there.

Sydney felt how his thrusts became harder, but his frequency also became slower. In a moment he would come, which excited Tina tremendously.

When Sydney came, Tina could clearly feel it, which made her tremble under her orgasm again. It felt absolutely great when Sydney reached for her breasts as if in a trance under his orgasm and kneaded them painfully, intensifying Tina's own orgasm under this pleasure pain.

Later, Sydney sat on a chair and alternately looked at the passing scenery, which could be seen only sparsely in the darkness, and then at Tina again.

"Where do you think you're going?", Tina wanted to know, enjoying the feeling of the sweat of pleasure on her body.

Sydney smiled. "Actually, just to see my friends. They've already flown ahead to the East Coast."

"And why didn't you fly with them?"

Sydney laughed. "Total fear of flying."

Tina laughed. "Now don't tell me you came to Australia on a ship."

Sydney shook his head. "No, that's where I flew. But don't ask me how I felt about it. And I had no interest in boarding another plane so soon. Especially not such a small machine. I'd rather take the train and get some rest."

Tina nodded with her lips pressed together. "Well, and there you go and land yourself a place with zero rest, since you now have to fuck me all the time."

Sydney raised his right eyebrow. "Really, all the time?"

"Of course. Social service to the elderly. And I think your break has been long enough. You really should take your commitment a little more seriously."

Sydney took a playfully resigned breath, pulled another condom out of the package, and walked over to Tina.